F is for Fireflies
God's Summertime Alphabet

By Kathy-jo Wargin

Illustrated by Linda Bronson

ZONDERkidz

A is for Anchor

Lift up your **A**nchor; the sunshine is here.
It's time for the blessings of God's summer cheer.

B is for Boat

Summer brings **B**oats
   that set sail in the breeze.
The water reminds us
   that God calms the seas.

C is for Castle

Let's find a beach
to build Castles of sand.
God tells us kindness
means lending a hand.

D is for Daisy

Let's pick some **D**aisies
of yellow and white.
The center reminds us
of God's pure delight!

E is for Everything

For God made the summer—he made Everything!
He made fish swim and whip-poor-wills sing.

F is for Fireflies

God made the Fireflies
light up the night,
a flash and a flicker—
his love is so bright!

G is for Garden

God made the **G**ardens,
and we help them grow,
weeding and watering
row after row.

H is for Hat

The sun rises high, and we feel very hot!
It's time for a **H**at and a cool shady spot.

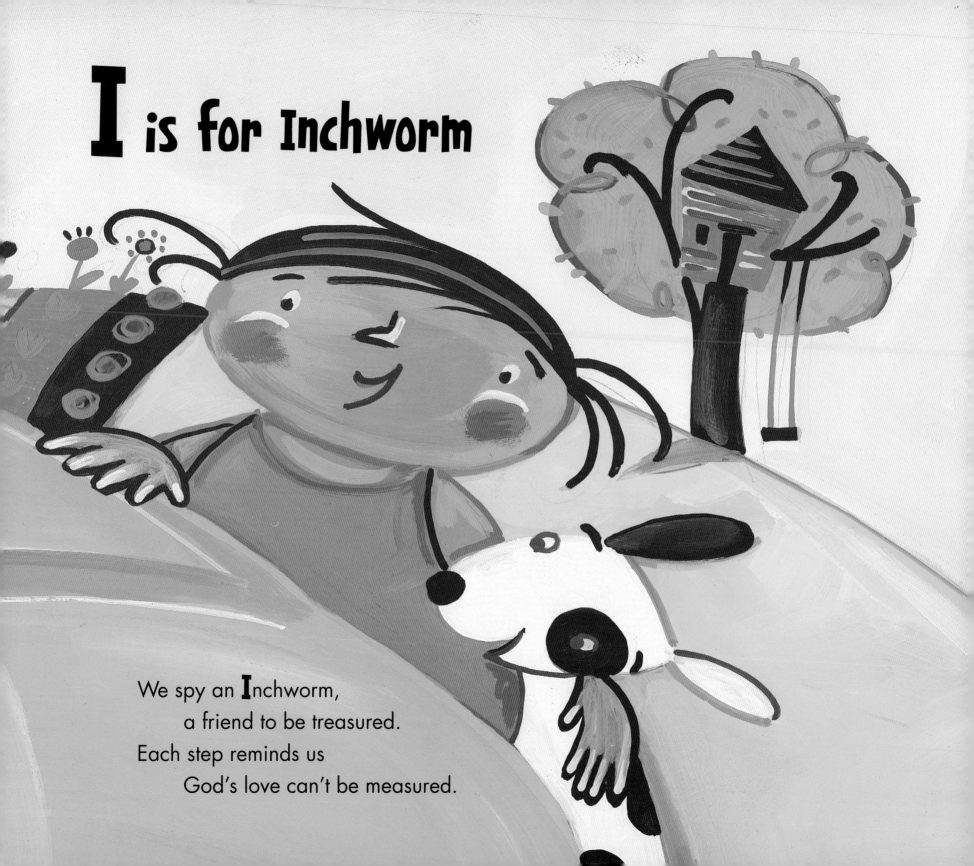

I is for Inchworm

We spy an Inchworm,
a friend to be treasured.
Each step reminds us
God's love can't be measured.

J is for Jump rope

It's time to Jump rope. Let's be quick on our feet.
We'll try to jump fast without skipping a beat.

K is for Kickball

Or we can play **K**ickball, a fun summer game.
We are all friends, and God knows us by name.

L is for Ladybug

Summer brings **L**adybugs
dressed up in spots.
Sometimes with few,
sometimes with lots!

M is for Meadow

Let's walk through the **M**eadow
and smell the fresh air.
Like wind through the grasses,
God's always there.

N is for Nature

In **N**ature we spot birds and blooms of each kind.
For God says look closer—just seek and you'll find.

O is for Owl

Owls perch high with their big watching eyes.
Remember that God wants us all to be wise.

P is for Picnic

It's time for a **P**icnic! Let's shout the news!
We'll spread out the blanket and kick off our shoes.

Q is for Quench

Let's **Q**uench our thirst
with fresh lemonade.
It always tastes better
when it is homemade.

R is for Rainbow

Rainbows in summer are God's way to say
that after the rain comes a brilliant new day.

S is for Swim

Let's go for a **S**wim—the water feels cool
when we jump in a lake or wade in a pool.

T is for Tire

Grandpa's old **T**ire swing
hangs from the tree.
A warm summer breeze
makes it fun to soar free.

U is for Universe

We sleep under stars
while admiring above,
the **U**niverse calling to all,
"God is love."

V is for Vacation

It's time for **V**acation—we've waited all year.
Wherever we travel, we know God is near.

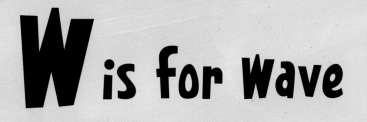

W is for Wave

Let's **W**ave to new friends as we travel along, and
make the time pass with a story or song.

X is for eXploring

We'll go eXploring;
　　there's so much to do—
hiking and biking,
　　enjoying the view.

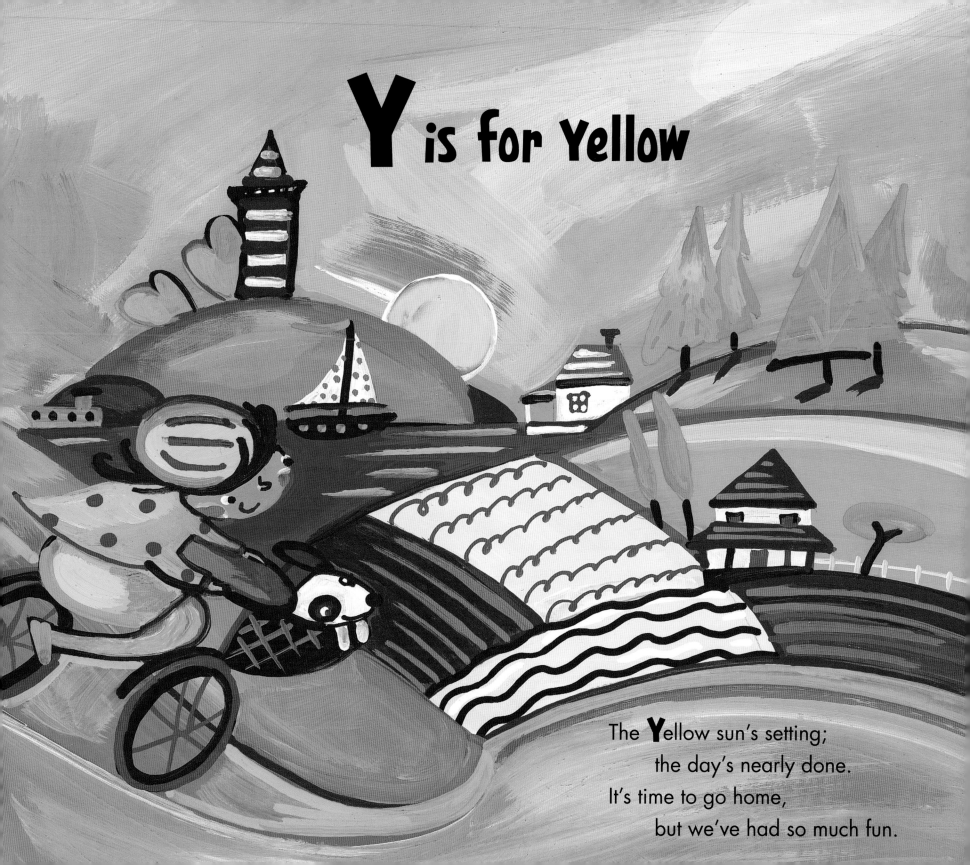

Y is for Yellow

The Yellow sun's setting;
the day's nearly done.
It's time to go home,
but we've had so much fun.

Z is for ZZZs

The hammock is waiting below the best trees.
Let's swing in the sunset before we catch **Z**ZZs.

From **A**nchors to **B**eaches
and summery things,
may you find the blessings that
God's summer brings.

To the spirit of summer and all the beauty it brings.
—K.W.

For Charlie and Frannie.
—L.B.

ZONDERKIDZ

F is for Fireflies
Copyright © 2011 by Kathy-jo Wargin
Illustrations © 2011 by Linda Bronson

This title is also available as a Zondervan ebook.
Visit www.zondervan.com/ebooks

Requests for information should be addressed to:
Zonderkidz, 3900 Sparks Dr, Grand Rapids, Michigan 49546

ISBN: 978-0-310-74418-4 (softcover)

Library of Congress Cataloging-in-Publication Data

Wargin, Kathy-jo.
    F is for fireflies / by Kathy-jo Wargin ; illustrated by Linda Bronson.
        p. cm.
        Summary: Presents rhyming sentences for each letter of the alphabet that remind
    the reader of God's blessings in summer.
        ISBN 978-0-310-71663-1 (hardcover)
        [1. Stories in rhyme. 2. Summer—Fiction. 3. God—Fiction. 4. Alphabet.]
    I. Bronson, Linda, ill. II. Title.
    PZ8.3.W2172Fai 2011
    [E]—dc22   2008044102

Editor: Barbara Herndon
Art direction: Jody Langley

Printed in China

14 15 16 17 18 19 /DSC/ 10 9 8 7 6 5 4 3 2 1